'LOVE' BIRDS ? OR 'ANGRY' BIRDS ?

(UNTOLD STORIES OF MILLENNIAL MARRIAGES)

NEELIMA DESHPANDE & LEENNA PARANNJPE

'Love' birds ? or 'Angry' birds ?

(Untold stories of Millennial Marriages)

Penned down By

Neelima Deshpande based on case studies of Leenna Parannjpe

©® Leenna Parannjpe

Leennaparannjpe@gmail.com

https://www.leennaparannjpe.com/

9920637522

©® Neelima Deshpande

neelima2002@gmail.com

https://www.blessedwriter.com/

7733025202

First Edition: 30 Mar,2022

Contents

Foreword

Introduction

Welcome to the journey of **'Love' birds** or **'Angry' birds**. In a fast evolving world, we experience certain changes in our marital bond which later result in frictions; the love seems diminishing, the magic seems disappearing and frictions become regular in daily life. We live in a modern world where we feel 'Soulmates', 'Made for each other' or 'Love birds' is what partners expect loving each other but it is not the reality.

It is the process and both the partners create this reality. Let's take you to the journey of millennial couples experiencing this process.

My name is Leenna Parannjpe and I will be leading you through this piece of writing. I have been married for the past 28 years and gone through many ups and downs of marriage. For other Marriage professionals it's a clinical perspective, but for me saving marriages is personal. 'My own life experiences acted as a catalyst in my decision of becoming a Marriage Coach.

I took a vow along with all the married couples, to guide them in their journey of Marriage. To make them realize Relationship Goals and discover passion over the years.'

Through The Rough Waters

When I say I relate to your stories it's because I have been on the same road you might be walking now. Belonging to a broken family and losing my spouse after a few years of marriage, taught me the toughest lessons of life. These experiences taught me to Not Give Up come what may. Today, I work for the betterment of married couple's lives'

I have a lovely husband and a daughter who is in her teens. Being a passionate and result-oriented professional with 25+ years of experience in providing Consultation, Coaching, Follow-up Sessions on Marriage Coaching, I provide the service with the key expertise in preventing a relationSHIP from sinking.

The focus of my professional career is in the creation of this book, designed for the millennials who want to grow and restore their companionship and love in their marriage. This book is for all millennials who plan to get married and want to understand what marriage is all about, and those who are already married, so that they can upgrade and improve their marriage.

By the end of the book, you will be able to recognize the core ingredients for a successful marriage, learn the necessary skills and techniques to tackle marital problems and challenges. Marriage coaching gives assured results.

- I am here to help you.
- Not to fix you.
- Change you or take responsibility of your actions.

Stories in this book will help you to understand :

- Knowing & understanding self marriage.
- Common marital issues Global Marriages face.
- And Ideas for repairing failed Marriage.

I have chosen this approach so that you can become aware, understand and put marriage in the right perspective. Not only will this book reveal how important communication, fair arguments, trust, forgiveness and love are in marriage, but it will also teach you the skills and techniques to combine these ingredients together to create your own successful version of marriage.

I will walk you through the personal experiences of these real life couples and the process they overcame their challenges with the help of coaching exercises, tips and smart actions.

You can contact me on https://www.leennaparannjpe.com/ This written piece is designed for everyone, regardless of whether you are married or not. All that is needed is your willingness and intention to understand and put marriage in the right perspective, uncover the secrets of a successful marriage and your readiness to bring in awareness into your relationship.

Feel free to learn, implement all the shared tips and I will be happy to see you on the other side!

Who this book is for:

This book is designed for every Dating / Engaged/ Unmarried /Married millennial.

ᐅᐅᐅ

This book is dedicated to my beloved late husband Sachin Ranadive

Leenna Parannjpe
Millennial Marriage Coach
Leennaparannjpe@gmail.com
https://www.leennaparannjpe.com/
9920637522

ᐅᐅᐅ

Preface

Preface / Forward

Welcome and thankful to all readers who are having this book in their hand. It's been enlightening journey to be associated with Millennial Marriage Coach **Leenna Parannjpe** madam.With initial few discussions only, professional bond between us got disappeared and new journey of enfolding layers of marital relationships started while briefing the points of case studies handled by Leennaji. Her attachment with all those who met her in this process is remarkable. It was reflecting while she was talking about them and taking care of all the professional ethics and etiquettes of not disclosing the client details.

In my previous personal and professional journey as a writer / blogger I wrote more than 1000 blogs comprises of Quotes, 100 word stories, Short stories, Poems. All this fiction based write up including Novel gave me satisfaction of self expression. In professional life, content development of educational and skill based programs widened my knowledge as well as developed me as a better person. Translating blogs from English and Hindi to Marathi language for various brands gave me the experience of working in a target based hours with higher accuracy.

This writing journey took a nice turn while working with Leennaji by changing my perspective towards martial issues. I am happy that she has chosen me to craft stories based on her case studies and express myself with full liberty with choice of words and writing style. All the points mentioned in stories are based on real life experiences leaving me less scope to change much in the story line except character and city names, professions, to hide the identity.Though we have taken all the precautions to change names of characters and cities and other necessary elements while writing each story, if any similarities found to you, it will be a mere coincidence. Without disturbing the theme, stories are written which are based on real life incidences.

I request you to read these stories as a case study and not personal opinions. If you read them in a broader context, I am sure it will help you out somewhere in life to gain some knowledge about handling relationships.

Neelima Deshpande
Writer, Blogger & HR Professional
neelima2002@gmail.com

1

'Angry' bird ? or love bird ?

"Though many of us like playing the game 'Angry bird' but that doesn't mean we will tolerate a life partner who is always shirty, furious and yelling at you on almost everything!"

Rima, started briefing me the reason why she wanted to separate from Amit, whom she was married and never happy after that due to his stubborn nature.

As Rima was in different mood and declaring the decision she had almost taken, I tried to understand her reason of approaching me in person.

In the discussion I came to know that, Amit told Rima in their 'honeymoon itself',

" I was not willing to marry you, but due to my parent's pressure, I am with you today in this marriage cage."

Further she revealed that, as they were not happy with each other and quarreled almost daily, they were not able to understand each other. This couple was having everything except happiness. Rima was an IT professional and Amit was working in a Marketing field. Though Rima was earning three times higher than Amit, she had never showed off her financial status to Amit.

It was her basic question to me,

"Is it not ok to live simple and sober life as I prefer? Is it necessary to go to pubs and attend parties and carry myself every time to impress others or rather Amit as he likes to do it? I am unable to convince him that one can enjoy the life in a simple way also."

With this, I found the exact clue what was missing in their arranged married life.

Rima was very introvert girl. 'kind of dry nature she is having!' was the complaint Amit had as she was not able to show the intimacy which he was expecting. Amit was very expressive guy with a lot of show buzz and out spoken personality. But when he received no response to his loving gestures, his anger burst out in a wrong manner being emotionally disturbed. He used Rima as a sex tool every time and slapped her once when he got angry. Rima forgave him for the first time.

Rima felt it's the common way of all husbands to get angry with wives and then without thinking of their mood, just rush to fulfill the physical need. Rima tried to adjust initially for few months. But she had broken when she saw Amit's orthodox parents supporting him every time. He simply used to join them to get refresh but what about Rima? All this led to the decision Rima was declaring to live separate.

Many times parents fail to make their child understand and teach to control the excess anger they carry every time. As a parent few things they might have not realized in childhood that what might be the consequences of not controlling a child at right age in a right manner.

Rima when calmed down, took sessions and worked upon herself to be emotionally strong, learnt to express and thought to give one more chance to their marriage. She declared Amit who was willing to get separate, firmly that she is not ready for the same and if Amit wished the same, she will file a case against him for domestic violence first and then only they will separate.

She was ready for the patch up only on these conditions that....

* He had to take the responsibility of his anger.
* Set some parameters which he had to follow to build their marriage.
* Never cross the set limit.

To give this chance to their marriage, initially they will have to live separately and not with his orthodox parents so that they both can give each other enough time to grow their marriage. Over pampered Amit, finally listened all her demands and fulfilled them as he felt some changes in Rima and realized that what he was willing, he was getting those beautiful changes in his wife.

Finally when they are happy with each other, I am happy too as I could save two love birds from getting separated.

2

Are marriages really made in heaven???

"If Marriages are really made in heaven, then why can't I experience it after a year of married life?"

Self doubted, Sapana was asking herself this question again and again since she is married to Hitesh, the only and very pampered son from a well off marawadi family. Though Sapana is MBA pass out, she had not done job before marriage and after marriage there was no scope left for her to do so. She was not having a liberty to even shut their bedroom in a day and even at night time. For every small petty things both Hitesh and Sapana needed to take permission from her mother in law.

Till now you might have understood that there was 'over indulgence' of one person (mother in law) who was hampering many lives at a time.

Sapana was very happy before her marriage. She had enjoyed freedom of speech and taken decisions earlier, on the contrary she had to beg for almost everything in her life after entering the lavish penthouse in Santacruz after marrying Hitesh. It was tough for a Napean sea resident elite class girl to understand that how can Hitesh tolerate over dominance of his mother in their married life too.

Before she could figure it out and seek help, just after enjoying at one party, Hitesh dropped her at her parent's home without telling any reason and blocked her everywhere in his life. She was banned from entering his home followed by a phone call by his mother asking for a divorce. In a fraction of seconds, everything collapsed living no hope of their reunion!

Keeping all this apart, Sapana started searching on net for any counselors' help. Finally after a few days struggle of rigorous search, she managed to find out my website to win the love life once again. With lots of love for life partner Hitesh and understanding his state of mind, that he might have been facing the same pressure by his over dominant mother, Sapana decided to help him rather than getting angry with him. When husband and wife become the support system for each other no one can stop them coming together.

The sessions began exploring new possibilities to gain Sapana's self confidence back. This is what exactly happened. With lots of Patience, courage and continued efforts taken as supported in the sessions by me, Sapana not only managed to enter in the home again but in their life too! within a span of two weeks.

Believe me I felt so proud of her!!!! Three months is too short period for anyone to regain the trust and acceptance which Sapana was able to do as Hitesh supported her by taking a stand for their married life privacy and decisions related to it.

'All is well that ends well.' Slowly Sapana and Hitesh won conversation held with parents and convinced them to start one more branch of their business in Singapore which Hitesh was taking care till now in India under his father's rule and guidance.

'A dream came true' like picture can be seen in Sapana's eyes when they were able to run the business successfully and reached to the happiest state of their marriage in Singapore.

3

Home sweet home.

Somewhere down in my mind, I always think of this line that says..."Home is not homely, if the people living inside it, aren't smiling!"

Mamata had similar kind of feeling after marriage, when she was shifted from Delhi to Mumbai. The very first reason for this was climatic change ! She was not used to humid weather so she felt tough to face it. Mamata was facing another major issue of keeping herself in 'Ghungat' all the time in humid weather. It was mandatory to keep pallu and ghungat while all the time. She was bit nervous in washing clothes by hands daily when not allowed to use washing machine just because her mother in law didn't like it and preferred hand wash. The list is long and it was never ending. It got increased day by day.

Mamata being a school teacher, had lots of patience. Her basic nature was also adjustable. So she tolerated all this up-to one year of her marriage.

She was missing all her old golden days when her boyfriend used to pamper her a lot. On her parent's advice she left him before marrying Ajit, a guy working in an IT firm and living a lavish life in Mumbai. Mamata accepted this relation wholeheartedly and made it clear to her boy friend and to herself also that she will be focusing on her new life only, after that day.

Then what, where and when it went so wrong that Mamta felt a need to get reconnected again with her old friend? You might be thinking what's new in it ? It is quite obvious! no certainly not !!! It is never obvious that someone will start liking or hating a person all of a sudden.

Mamata left Ajit. She was not ready to come back. Ajit was having his own super ego which was not allowing him to introspect. He was rather asking himself,

"What Mamata did not get in my house which she needed in her life. Money, lavish life, good looking and well off husband....what someone needs more than that? And there is no big deal if she cared my family members as this is what she is supposed to do after marriage."

As per him, he is earning a lot and giving his presence in the home at late night and leaving home early in the morning should be accepted. It is ok to move out of the home without sharing his feelings or showing loving gesture to his wife.

On the top of it, he suspected Mamata without consulting with her and traced her phone calls. All this resulted in leaving him and not because she was willing to join her boyfriend. She was feeling lonely. So she had started talking to her friend which was mistaken in another direction by Ajit.

Everything is possible. One can rejoin the broken hearts again if they really wish to do it with lots of understanding and patience which were shown by Ajit in our discussions. He approached me through my website suggested by his family friend.

Ajit was able to win Mamata's heart as she was dying for his love, word of appreciation and respect in his eyes for her. She felt that somewhere her mother in law is not willing to change much. So they both started living in another flat nearby to family.

For a year long time span, they were not able to know each other as they never had that opportunity. So they spent lot of time together after that and now they are living a happy life as a parent of one year kid.

4

My heart is beating.

"My heart is beating, keeps on repeating.....I am waiting for you.....time is fleeting, time is fleeting.....time is...."

Atul who was never in any serious relationship, happily and anxiously waiting for his bride to enter the room on their first night. But obvious, they got very less time to interact with each other and mingle to gel with each other's feelings in these two days period after their marriage. An IT guy from Pune based well known firm when got married with very creative minded Reva who was having her boutique in Nasik, had rare opportunities to meet or know each other before their arranged marriage took place.

"Unnecessary hurries in few things will surely lead to worries in life..." Atul and Reva's case which I handled was the best example of it. Within a week Atul contacted me through one of his reference asking very straight question to me,

"Mam, tell me where I am wrong? Is it something not expected to have strong desire to get intimate with your wife? Why am I getting alleged for the same by Reva and her mother?"

Thinking in a mind, I tried to figure it out quickly. In prima facie, nothing seems wrong to point out but there was something which led all this....

After going into the root while discussing it, what I found is, real culprit was 'Reva's mother.' Reva used to listen to her mother's preaching, that she should not entertain any kind of injustice in her married life. To check whether everything is going smoothly or not, her mother used to call up Reva many times. Getting every smallest bit of information and feeding her it's would be repercussions, led to the conclusion that the guy means Atul is very aggressive and just using Reva for his physical needs.

"What?" Yes this was my response too! When I heard it.

Basically there was a need of developing feelings for each other's first and then enter into next level of married life. But before Atul could understand this from someone or on his own, his actions of showing his love were mistaken by Reva.

The very first thing I asked him to say "sorry" to Reva and start dialogue with her to become her best friend first. This worked well along with other things which he did with his full patience and determination to get Reva back in his life. Within 15 days time Atul and Reva were comfortable with each other as Reva's mother also took few sessions to understand why it is necessary now, to give Reva and Atul their space.

Needless to say that Atul and Reva are now my big fans and share my contact number to all newly married friends in their peer group whom they found the need of it.

5

All is well that ends well!

After a year of successful married life, Samar and Reva are so happy every time when they thank me as a marriage coach and not a counselor. As per them, without the sessions they took from me, marriage was never thought of so easy and happy by them.

Cutting the long story short, When emotional compatibility was checked before entering into married life by Reva and Samar, in the planned sessions, their marriage is bound to happen successful in every ups and downs. Samar was quite impressed by the way he was taken out from the disaster in his love marriage planned with Shweta before this marriage taking place with Reva.

Bangalore based Samar who was working in MNC and on his parent's wish was searching a suitable match for him, met Shweta in one common trekking group. After spending almost a year together in virtual relationship where mere chatting with each other took place a lot and hardly they met each other in three trecks and still finalized that they are the perfect match for each other.

With this confidence, Samar opened up with his parents and convinced them for his inter-cast marriage with Shweta. Everything was set but not the bride! She blocked him all of a sudden and started avoiding him. After so many tryouts to reach but failed, Samar somehow managed to get my contact details. He contacted me for seeking the help in understanding Shweta's psychology. He was afraid what will he do if after marriage also she behaved like this. Our session journey started to understand their relationship.

Initially, he was unaware of the facts that she was already engaged with one muslim guy who was ready to marry with her. His parents permitted him but Shweta's parents were reluctant. So she thought to pretend that she is ready to marry with Samar a new match she found for herself. After marrying with Samar, her plan was to spend minimum time required to get divorce and join her old beloved muslim friend again, whose parents were ready to accept her happily at any point of time.

Are you Shocked ? the same was my reaction too! when I came to know this from Shweta herself. When along with Samar, I visited her office to trace why she is not willing to face him, she revealed this truth to me.

It's but natural that Samar lost his temper but he managed his cool after discussing all truth and what kind of a trap was planned for him by Shweta. He thanked for saving him. Samar was having faith on me as he had taken few sessions to understand what's happening to him and his marriage when Shweta was not responding him initially.

Samar and his wife Reva thanked many times to me for making them understand that marriages proved nice and happy when planned on emotional grounds by doing compatibility checks and deciding the purpose of why someone wants to get married?

It was easy to understand him as he had practically understood in his case that many times girls are taking undue advantages now a days, knowing law is supporting them. They are using marriage as a tool which is indeed a sad part.

In Samar's case, all these stages were avoided as Shweta finally realised and accepted that her plan was different from what she was pretending to Samar. Many lives were saved from facing emotional trauma leading to happy ending, and saying 'All is well that ends well !'

6

Absence makes the heart grow fonder.

—♡—

When people we love are not with us, we love them even more ! Priti in a confused state of mind, was trying to co relate the proverb she was reading in a book with her own life while sitting in court.

"Well Priti, if this is your final decision, I am also searching a good lawyer for myself now! I was waiting for you till date and I will still wait for you. My doors and heart will always welcome you, if you think to return at any moment till we see each other in court!"

Samar was talking to his wife Priti. He was very disheartened with his wife Priti and her elder sister Payal who was once his colleague and best friend too.

" Priti, no need to go anywhere. Not for any compromise or to meet the marriage coach with Samar. Our decision is final that, you will be living with me. I will take care of you. Samar is well off, he will be paying you good amount even if you get separated from him"

Payal had taken the decision on behalf of Priti as she was used to do it always. Payal and Priti were sisters. Being elder than Priti, for almost 10 years, Payal was always over protective and dominating while taking decisions for Priti. It was wholeheartedly accepted by Priti too. When all doors were closed by Priti and Payal, Samar visited me alone as he was truly in love with Priti and wished to save their marriage which was on the verge of breaking.

" I need your help to understand what went wrong from my side in our marriage. I had lost my mother due to cancer. After her death also, Priti had many issues with her. She is always in a complaining mood and mode while talking to me. Not ready to forget anything happened in the past between her and my mother. I discussed this with Payal too as Priti listens her and obeys too! After our marriage also she used to brief everything with Payal, which was against my wish. Priti told about this planned visit with you to Payal and then all actions were taken faster than before. They had sent me divorce notice. I tried to discuss with Payal, but she doesn't seem to be interested in resolving our issues, rather adding fuel to fire. Now, she is not allowing Priti to talk with me."

After a yearlong period Samar was sitting in front of me and telling me all about his life.

" I asked you to take few compatibility check sessions before you get into this marriage. You both are totally different personalities. You are too practical where as Priti is an extremely emotional girl. She can't come out of the bitter phases she has faced. Similarly I told you to stay away from Payal too! Irrespective of your best friendship, you had chosen Priti as your life partner. Payal and you were best friends for years and working together. You both were comfortable as a friend. Being practical by nature you and Payal perceive the things similarly where as Priti perceives them differently.

I was trying to remind him and taking more points from his discussion to help him.

" Yes, I remember that. It was our mistake to enter into married life before understanding each other or setting some parameters of handling each other's needs. Actually when Payal, gave her consent for our marriage, we thought we can manage it. We were running short of time also. My mother was not well. So hurriedly we took the decision.

Payal and I were having nice bonding. She was elder than me, but being practical by nature we never felt that age difference in our very close friendship. Priti was emotional, sensitive, very obedient and respectful with Payal, so I liked her personality traits which were not in me and Payal too! But at the time of handling, I forgot to take expert's help to maintain the happiness in our marriage by understanding each other better.

I can't spend much time or I can't be so close with Payal, as I used to be before my marriage with Priti who is very emotional. I can't handle her too much sensitiveness. I am totally alone now, without my mother, wife and best friend!"

As a coach, I helped him to come out of that phase and face the situation. He is still waiting and working on saving his marriage. Priti who is still unable to take decision on her own, depends upon Payal to tell the next lead.

Needless to say Payal who was missing her best friend, and feeling jealous of her own sister, is still willing to see her friend. If she is unable to get Samar back in her life, she will make everyone unhappy.

Weird and strange too! But it's true, when one is blind in selfishness, can reach to any extreme! Better to take preventive steps than to repent in the future.

7

An apple a day !

———•♡•———

'An apple a day, keeps the doctor away !' is much known proverb to all of us.

Equally known was the fun made by all friends, to the doctor couple Sudhir and Ragini when they were madly together spending time with each other.

Sudhir did his MD and Ragini had completed BDS before they tied a knot with each other. Sudhir's both the parents were also doctors and much similar to his nature of being social and expressive.

No one noticed including Sudhir that Ragini is less expressive or participate less in the conversations held between them. Sudhir being the independent child was brought up to take decisions resulted in having good decision making ability as his mother was having. They were so fast in taking actions or responding to situations and always had their say as they could express themselves well.

A year passed like this and finally in few arguments Ragini felt that not an apple but Sudhir's pinching words were keeping her away from him. Like usual partners have differences between them, Sudhir and Ragini also had, but they were taking different turns.

Differences between them were not getting solved after discussion but rather used to get converted into serious quarrels which used to last for weeks. Sudhir had a habit of making comments or passing his opinions in bitter words. Being practical natured guy, for him it's a part of that hot conversation and nothing more than that.

On the contrary, Ragini who was a emotional soul, used to take his each word to her heart. She was sticking to that particular word which was used in a wrong manner and got upset due to that. She was able to calm down herself unless discussed it to get satisfactory results which she never had.

Ragini had only one person in that home i.e. daughter, whom she was feeling comfortable. Ragini was very much possessive for her and was not allowing anyone to get more attached to her. Ragini took care of everything and somewhat obsessed with over hygiene and cleanliness.

Every couple is having their own language of understanding each other. In this case it was badly missing. Sudhir who used to get carried away in his debating arguments with Ragini, never felt that she also had her opinion and needed to be given time as she was not habitual to act as fast as he or his mother.

Being slow or less expressive person, Ragini's need to share her opinion never came in his mind until she left the home with her daughter and decided not to return in his life again.

In the quench of saving his married life Sudhir managed to find my website, through his friend who was living in his colony in Bangalore. In the sessions taken by him, he gave his best to take small actions first, which were indicating that he really wished to be with Ragini.

With his understanding gestures and active ear given to understand what real happiness meant for Ragini, he was able to take her back in his life and their sweet home in Bangalore. Sudhir is still working on improving his lack of connectivity issue with Ragini and living together with parents without giving a feeling that all are in one group and Ragini is left alone.

Sometimes we have everything except the quality time to spend with each other. Being in the profession which was much in demand in the covid situation, all were having tight and stressful schedules. When we are able to give that feeling of inclusiveness, everything is possible even to win a heart again which was lost in the busy life. This can bring back ease and happiness in your married life.

8

Is everything fair in the marriage?

When you have an arranged marriage, many things will be taken care by seniors in the home or by parents. When you have a love marriage, you take the onus on your shoulder but what if, the marriage is arranged marriage and still the onus is on your shoulders?

Why puzzled? Marriage whether it is love or arranged or arranged love the onus will always lie on your shoulders. If husband and wife are strong enough to handle every ups and downs in the life together, they are bound to be leading happy married life.

Through one online marriage portal, Meenal and Yash met each other. After feeling compatible for each other they had decided to enter in married life so conveyed their 'yes' for each other to parents. As parents were involved in it from day one, they were ready for marrying with each other. Yash's mother was keeping a watch on Meenal's every small act leading to lots of observations and interference in Meenal's life.

As Yash and Meenal were happy with each other, initially Meenal neglected these things. But later when her sister in law was also getting involved with her mother in law and continuously suggesting changes, she felt uncomfortable.

Yash was younger in the home. His sister got married before eleven years but her say was still there in the family. It's like a strong buddies they were acting in every situation. So Meenal asked Yash to discuss this matter with his mother and sister.

For Yash these were not much serious things so he postponed it for the future which never arose. After their marriage also Meenal requested him lot many times that she is a responsible person, working as a Financial Analyst in a big firm and a wife of a equally responsible partner working in

MNC.

So when every time she used to get instructions for what to wear, what to eat, when to do and what not to do, it hampered her mood and affected her professional life many times.

Meenal also made him realised that for her, the situation is getting worst. Father in law is a depression patient, mother in law is over dominating and sisiter in law is focusing more in their life instead of her own. She finally told Yash straight away,

" I am not able to tolerate all the time nagging by both of them now, so you should speak with them."

Yash who was not much serious about this, started avoiding the situation as usual. In that hot exchange of words in loud voices rose which made Yash's father panic.

In one extremely angry moment, Meenal slapped Yash. Situation got worst which could be resolved but no one was in the mood. Physical violence was never justified so Yash was not ready to forgive her instantly. Her father in law called up police. This pattern was getting repeated after that, as no one was able to resolve the root issue.

Whenever father in law felt insecure due to the couple's regular fight, he used to call police. Finally Meenal returned her maternal home. She was having lots of patents on her name but now her career was at stake due to family issues.

Yash on the recommendation by his friend, visited my website and with changed mindset he decided to give second chance to his relationship. In the discussions held, he realized slowly that Meenal also had her side and being a wife she was having some expectations from him.

She had discussed the issue before their marriage, so that everything would lead to smooth road. Sometimes small things make big differences in marriage, and it matters a lot.

Yash also realized meanwhile that his family was not much bothered for him as his mother asked him to move out from the home once and Meenal supported him that day irrespective of their current separated situation. She was able to win Yash's confidence once again to the extent where they came together and started living in the flat nearby to Yash's family.

Meenal also took efforts on controlling her anger. Currently as a happy parent of one year child, Meenal and Yash are staying peacefully and proved that everything is possible in the marriage.

When your relationship can lead to breaking situation, correct steps taken at right time, with the help of right person like experts / marriage coach, marriage can be enjoyed once again too.

9

A chain is only as strong as its weakest link.

"When we take care of the weakest portion of anything, we can enjoy the strongest part automatically. Let's apply the same principle in marriage! What do you think is the weakest part of your married life?"

As a marriage coach, I was asking Savitha who approached me to take professional help in understanding and making her married life happy and better forever.

"Umm...well there are many, as per every person's opinion but understanding is one of them which plays a vital role in making it successful or disaster!" Savitha replied as per her personal experience.

"True, then what do you think was the weakest link in your marriage? Same thing ?? Understanding between you two?? Or something else?"

I raised next question to ponder Savitha.

"A year ago I got married with Rohan from Nagpur. We spent almost 5 years together before marriage, when we were working in the same firm. We invested that precious time to understand each other and convince our parents too that we are perfect match for each other. Initially my parents were not ready but later Appa and Amma were happy with my decision. They planned a grand wedding for us as per my in laws' wish. So I don't think that understanding was an issue between us. I mean, between me and Rohan."

Savitha shared her opinion.

"Ok, that's good ! Then tell me why Rohan is not ready to take you to his home again? Why did you leave him and return to Chennai? Just think over it again and then reply." I was trying to get some more points from her so that actual cause could be identified.

" Rohan, and me were very happy till first year of our marriage. We both were working, so most of our time was spent outside and we were hardly able to spend time with his family. So it was easy for me to ignore many comments made by his mother and sister on my accent and colour. But later I found that it was done purposely and his father also joined them.

It was kind of a competition between me and Rohan's sister they had created. In every task done by us they were doing comparison and making fun of me. Rohan changed his job so we were not able to spend time together. In lockdown, things got worst. While doing my job of an 'Operational analyst, I found it hard for me to balance my work effectively and ignore their comments."

Savitha finally gave lot many points and evidences what she had gone through.

" Have you shared this with Rohan? What was his role in it? Was he supportive?" I asked to conclude to some point.

" No, actually not. He was a different person that whom I loved and married. He was not ready to listen against his family. One day in argument, with my mother in law, I raised my voice too. She was not expecting it from me. That argument went in a wrong direction leading her to raise her hand on me and physically abusing me which was very insulting for me. I took it as an alarming bell. So I also exchanged harsh bitter words with her and left home in anger. But now I can't live without Rohan, so I am talking to you."

" I can understand what you have gone through. We can still make this marriage happening and happy. Your communication with Rohan must be initiated at first. He will be ready to speak with you only if he thinks that you respect his family. This is not the time to decide who was wrong? Relations get spoiled with ego. Your in- laws are elder than you, so lead to say sorry to them. We will work upon your anger management and rebuild your relationship with Rohan to make it the same as it was earlier."

Savitha did the same as suggested. She also took few more sessions till she won Rohan's heart again and made him understand his role in her life and what exactly she needs in terms of support from him.

Rohan who was matured enough to understand that his mother is not going to change so soon, took the decision of living separately near to his parents so that he can save his marriage, can develop a strong bond with Savitha first and help Savitha to understand his family. He became a strong bridge between his family and Savitha till they understand each other's expectations and fulfill them smoothly.

Everything is possible when one decides. It's always easy to join hands with each other than to break hearts and suffer lifetime.

21

10
Couple or Just Paying Guest?

Any kind of extremity will always lead to some issues. But we fail to understand it unless faced the situation as it happened with Reena, our heroine in this story.

Reena, a good looking and intelligent girl, working in IT field went to Germany for official onsite project just after 6 months of her marriage with Suraj the only son of his parents. Reena was practical in her every approach be it professional or personal. On the other hand Suraj was very soft spoken and emotional guy. Being well mannered and well educated, person, Suraj reached on the top in his professional life soon after taking care of CRM profile in his early days.

As Reena and Suraj both were matured and career oriented, smooth shifting from India to Germany took place in Reena's case. They both were in contact with each other on Skype whenever possible in her two year's stay there.

Communication has a major role especially when you are in distant relationships. Somehow Reena and Suraj had some issues with each other. Suraj was very particular in choosing words and their usage with proper tone for himself and family pride was at the highest importance. Whereas Reena was casual and very practical in her thoughts which had created a hurdle in their communication held on Skype.

Somehow her project got over and she returned to India and thought that it will be all ok as it was in initial days where they actually were in goody goody relation. Somehow her expectations failed badly when Suraj asked her to return to her parent's home and never to return back. It was a massive blow for her where she wished to introspect what actually caused this. In that try she got my contact number and my website link.

In the discussions held she strongly showed her desire to work upon her tone, words and over all her communication style. With her great efforts she managed to win his heart where he was ready to stay with her in a separate flat away from their parents. But unfortunately this also didn't work for a long.

In the flat they were living in such a manner as paying guests. They stopped talking to each other and started taking care of themselves on their own without depending upon each other. Below one roof, when husband and wife lived in solitude, Reena felt it was her turn to take the lead more rigorously.

She found every small task where they could come together, or cross each other where at least they had eye contacts. It was very difficult to win Suraj as he was not responding initially but hard ship pays. Finally with lots of improved communication skills and efforts Reena won his heart again.

In lockdown Suraj lost his job but as he was financially sound, he worked out a plan for starting up his own venture in Canada. He has lots of friends already staying there, so it was easy for him to think about it. Very soon Suraj and Reena are planning to move to Canada and enjoy their food business. Reena is also happy to give a new start while handling her IT job in Canada along with Suraj.

11

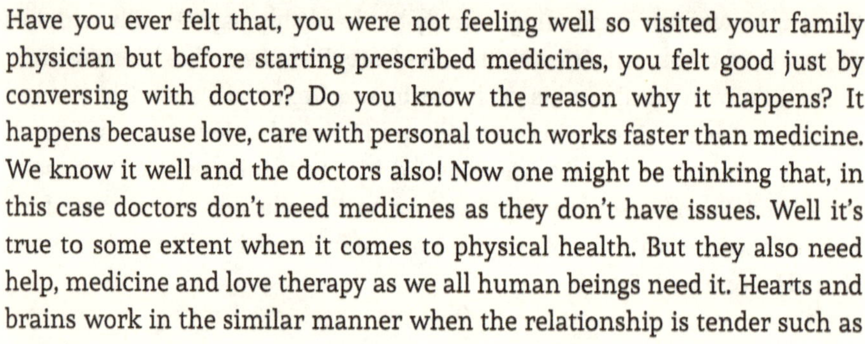

Love, Beyond Medicines.

Have you ever felt that, you were not feeling well so visited your family physician but before starting prescribed medicines, you felt good just by conversing with doctor? Do you know the reason why it happens? It happens because love, care with personal touch works faster than medicine. We know it well and the doctors also! Now one might be thinking that, in this case doctors don't need medicines as they don't have issues. Well it's true to some extent when it comes to physical health. But they also need help, medicine and love therapy as we all human beings need it. Hearts and brains work in the similar manner when the relationship is tender such as marriage.

Dr. Sohan and radiologist Sarita tied a knot with each other but failed to forget their first life partners from their first bitter marriage experience. One has to move ahead in the life and try to forget bitter past so that it will not hamper present and future both. Dr. Sohan tried to accept it initially but reluctant to have child. Sarita on the other hand not being rigid, was still struggling with her past experiences to forget. The present similar experiences were compelling her to compare every now and then.

Her relationship with her mother in law was not so cordial enough. Somehow these things got stretched to that extent where Dr. Sohan was not willing to adjust anymore with Sarita. He lost his self control and became an alcoholic person.

Needless to say, when you caught up in a wrong habits, you failed to remember that you have everything in life. Lavish bungalow, bank balance, good educational degree and honor all this was in vain for him when he couldn't find the love, affection from Sarita. He shifted to different bedroom. Sarita was trying hard to manage with him as well as his mother. In his anger Dr. Sohan was physically violent with Sarita which was not tolerated by her. Her profession was at stake. She was not able to concentrate on her work.

Sohan's mother was emotionally and financially dependent on him. Being a simple living but orthodox by nature, she was having her own expectations from daughter in law. After her husband's death she was more clinging to Dr. Sohan. Finally when Sarita failed to manage all, she with her parents help, got my reference and visited me to take sessions to help herself out.

It's bit difficult when there is a loss of connectivity in life partners so very first efforts were taken by Sarita to find that connection with her mother in law.

Basically mother in law was willing few rituals to be followed which were not implemented by Sarita. Sarita with her sister was brought up in a different atmosphere where these things were not bounded on them forcefully. So with little conscious efforts Sarita won her mother in laws heart. She started dressing up differently on festivals, took blessings from mother in law and started taking pallu whenever possible. This had generated a bond between them but still Dr. Sohan was reluctant on his decision which broke Sarita's heart and she left home.

She talked with her mother in law about her desire to have a child and also discussed that it's against her self esteem to stay with them as she took lots of efforts to change herself but did not receive anything in return. She left home and shifted in PG. Within a month, Dr. Sohan realized his mistake that he is stretching it unnecessarily and it's time for him to change also.

He took Sarita back in his life and also in the home. The shift in their mindset was permanent. He took care of Sarita, supported and encouraged her to appear in next exams to have professional growth. In their personal life also, Dr. Sohan showed the interest of having a baby and they both took a couple decision. In Sarita's pregnancy, he was focused on her health care and behaved so well as one has to be in that phase.

Life takes turns, put us in situations where one may think, it's the end, but if we have courage to be flexible and do some changes in ourselves for better life experiences we are bound to get them.

12
Just For you Dear!

"It will be better Sarita, if you can wind up all your handover formalities in office. We need to focus on your marriage preparations now. Raghav's family is well known in Patana and you should match up with their family members in dressing and culture."

Sarita's mother was talking to her daily and trying to teach her daughter how to be flexible while adjusting in new atmosphere after marriage.

"Didi, get ready for Raghav's marriage. I am happy today that I have kept my word that I will take care of your little son Raghav and you all in your illness, with my two sons throughout my life. That made me to stay with you after my husband's death which was helpful for our both the families."

Kajal, who was a real sisiter of Raghav's mother i.e. his mausi was talking to his mother who was struggling with her last stage cancer.

"Sarita, I am very close to my mother, and you can see that she is in her last stage so we should be giving her most of time. I am not compelling you but trying to say you that, kindly excuse me if I am paying more attention to her after our marriage too."

Raghav expressed his innermost feelings with some fear in mind about his mother's health to Sarita. Both gave their most of the time to her and made her last days joyful and satisfactory. But as destiny has it's own plan, after 3 months of Raghav's marriage, his mother passed away leaving him in deep grief.

"Sarita, now charge of this house is in my hand. So make sure that I should get equal respect as you were giving to my Didi"

Kajal reminded Sarita, when she felt that Sarita was taking few decisions in kitchen and trying to look after home more than before. Sarita was ok with it. Basically she was not behind any power. But sometimes she felt it's beyond the power war. She felt that there is some kind of strong bond and soft corner between her father in law and Raghav's mausi.

"Raghav, I know it's a great emotional loss for you as you had lost your mother. But it's almost a year passed to our marriage and few things are really bothering me. I think you need to be firm being the only son of your father."

Sarita tried to talk to Raghav whenever it was possible to her but she couldn't reveal him the tender relationship between his father and his mausi. Neither she could express her pain and verbal abuse and domination initially by Raghav's mausi followed by his sons too. With some valid reason she went to Mumbai where she expressed this to her parents.

" I am sorry mummy but I think, I will not be able to tolerate any torture anymore now. Many times I felt it is being done purposefully so that I should leave that home" Sarita was telling all to her mother when her father also joined the discussion.

" I can tell you lot of incidents how my life got changed after my mother in law's death. Raghav's father has his say in the family and Raghav couldn't utter a single word in front of him."

After listening to Sarita, her parents decided to find some expert's advice so they find my website and took Sarita to me. In the sessions held with me, Sarita shared all what she shared with her parents.

" I think the bond between you both has not yet developed. You were together forbade year but not able to spend enough time to build a trust. Basically Raghav may or may not be knowing the truth about relationship you have observed in a short span of your stay there. It is more important to support Raghav on emotional end where he will feel closer to you. He needs courage to stand in front of his father. Then only he will able say something. For that you need to go to Patana and try to win his heart first and then together you can convince the family that you will be living separately. As per their wish they are willing the same but not taking the lead keeping their status in the society."

Many discussions were held were Sarita made up her mind to go to Patna again. Similarly lot of efforts were taken to build Raghav's courage. Slowly but firmly they took decision to live separately and now enjoying their life as if they are just married forgetting the past bitter experiences.

13

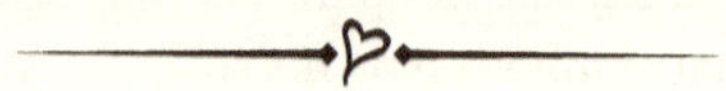

I still miss someone!

"There's someone for me somewhere...and I still miss someone...."

Sai was humming Johnny Cash's most famous song in a solitude. After marriage when she left India and joined her husband Sagar in US she was feeling lonely many times. Sagar reached home and announced her that,

" Sai, Let's move out and chill with friends. There is new outlet opened in the mall near by Rocky's house. So he has invited us and I have given my consent on our behalf." As Sai was not replying, he asked the same thing again.

" Sorry Sagar, I don't wish to go out with friends anymore or not even willing to visit any outlets. I am fade up of this!" Sai replied but Sagar astonished by it.

" What ! You are fade up of going out? then why were you complaining to your and my parents that I don't take you out or don't give time. I am busy with my work only! What does all this mean to you? I made today's plan to cheer you up after knowing it from my parents about your mood. You just pretend something different to them and your behavior is totally different from it. You need to change a lot !"

Sagar got angry when he was saying this all. Sai felt bad looking at his body language and replied in the same manner as he has spoken with her,

" No, I will not change now anymore! Rather you need to change your temperament now. I left my prestigious job as a CA in good firm. Left my parents, relatives, dear friends and moved next moment with you here in the US. I was having faith that you will fulfill all my dreams by being my best friend in this new world. You will take care of my emotions. But you are not yet simply connected with me. Then how can I expect more from you?"

Sagar got confused what to reply but still he murmured,

" All girls do the same thing, what's big deal in it? and I haven't stopped you from doing job? Then what are you blaming me for financial security? Am I not giving you money? In fact I insisted and sent you many times for shopping by handing over my credit cards permanently to you. But you don't like going out alone! What should I do? Shall I leave my job and sit at home with you?" Basically I don't like our internal things going out, which you have done by discussing all with our parents."

" What's wrong in it Sagar? They are our parents and they have right to know about us! We are here away from our country. They and even I feel happy while talking to each other. That's my upbringing! You have taken your decisions on your own till now it's good but you forget to take others into consideration while doing so. I do agree that all girls do that. But I don't agree that, 'It's not a big deal!' It is total transformation we are going through! But you will never understand it!"

Sai left the hall and went to Kitchen helplessly. She was not willing to hurt Sagar but unknowingly she did, she felt so as she was very caring and emotional girl. On the other hand Sagar was disappointed as his plan for going out got cancelled and Sai spoke many things which he never thought she will.

After a thoughtful conversation with her parents and few friends of her age, Sai decided to take professional help to sort this out. She wanted to find someone who would listen to her story and not judge her. She found me and wanted to book the consultation with me.

"Marriages need some time to ripen as mango pickle does! These are initial days where one needs to spend as much time with newly life partner as he or she can. For a being one can take lead and responsibility to make that relationship strong. In your case, if Sai, you are ready then we can do wonders in your marriage. Luckily you both don't have any complicated issues. These are just connectivity failure issues."

I was giving hope to Sai which was much needed at that time. She was very hardworking and willing to support in every sense to make her relationship healthy with Sagar. In few sessions she could able to express herself well to Sagar that,

" I am looking forward to your time and attention for me and not just outings. I wish that we should plan our weekends combine and not that you plan as per your wish and convenience every time and we are with lot many people always. There is need to spend some time which will be totally only for each other so that we can understand each other better. These days will never come again so I am not running behind job immediately but at the same time I feel that I should be financially independent."

Late, but slowly Sagar could understand Sai better with these kind of patient dialogues done with him. When he realised he agreed with Sai by confessing,

" You were right Sai. I failed initially understanding your core desires and mistook your words. I am feeling sorry for it. Here after, I promise you that I will also try to change myself. We will plan together whenever and wherever possible. I will be with you always. You will not feel lonely here now! I can understand your need of having dialogues with dear ones. I will start it soon and I will never stop you to do the same!"

What else a happy marriage needs other than the understanding and supporting nature of your partner ! Just connected feeling needs to be developed in the initial days of marriage to make it a heaven.

14

Who's Onus lies on the shoulder?

" What do you mean by this that who's onus lies on my shoulder? "

Dr. Gauri was asking me as she got confused with my question while our discussion was going on. To achieve the motive of our planned visit with her I asked that question as a millennial marriage coach to her in the beginning of discussion only. Further I asked her,

" Gauri, do you really love Manish and want to continue this marriage or do you have some different plans for your life? "

This made Gauri more puzzled. In a confused state of mind she replied,

" Madam, why will I have my own different plans or why will I think of leaving my beloved husband Manish? We haven't even spent much time together after our marriage. I could live there only for fifteen days and then I left him to take care of my father who is suffering from paralysis. Manish knows this all and his parents too!"

I got a thread to turn the discussion in more effective direction so that without hurting Dr. Gauri she will herself understand what went wrong in her marriage. She was so much engrossed in fulfilling duties that she was unable to find the loophole which made her plans for married life suspicious. I clearly discussed with her why Manish asked me to meet her once,

"Gauri, I hope you are unaware of what Manish is going through these days! What I guess after meeting you is that you are very emotional and caring person. Your nature will not allow you to hurt anyone on purpose and that's the reason we are meeting here today to resolve the issues between you and Manish if there are any!"

I then asked Manish to express his feelings in his words to Gauri and me once again which he told me in previous sessions taken by him to clear his confusion whether his decision of marrying Dr. Gauri was correct or not? I asked the same thing to Manish and he tried to express,

" Me and Gauri met in a common group of our mutual friends. After liking each other, we decided to get married and so proceeded for our parent's permission for the same. We are lucky to have understanding parents so they accepted our relation and we got married happily.

Everything was going smoothly till that. Me as a CA by profession and Gauri as a doctor were having tight job schedules where spending time with each other was difficult. To give us our time to mingle in the initial days of our marriage, my parents showed understanding and went to live with my elder brother in another city..."

After that Manish kept quiet for a while so Gauri continued further by telling that,

" Yes, they told us that. They are very supportive. They were planning to live there for few more months. Manish and I was planning to see Bhaiya's new born baby girl and return together with Manish's parents. But unfortunately I was stuck up with my hospital duties so badly that to take care of my father I went to maternal house on 16th day of my marriage."

While Gauri was telling this to us, her eyes shown some realization. Very politely she accepted that she was not able to give time to Manish and his family members. She then discussed with Manish in front of us only.

" I am really sorry Manish for taking things granted and neglecting you all who are very supportive and understanding people. But tell me frankly, what should I do? This is my responsibility. I can't leave my father in this state and turn my back to my professional life too. As a doctor I have this responsibility and when I said this you are asking who's onus I am carrying on my shoulder? Our parents are our responsibility, don't you agree with me?" To conclude it on a positive note, on behalf of Manish I explained Dr. Gauri that,

"Indeed our parents are our responsibility and to take care of our professional responsibilities we need to be prompt and specially in the medical profession. But it is equally important to take care of personal responsibilities in newly married life and priorities few things in a different manner. These initial days after marriage will never come again with the same feelings for each other. "

Gauri asked a suggestion to solve her issue of prioritizing things. Manish gave her solution by backing his words why he said that Gauri is carrying other's onus on her shoulder.

" Gauri, with due respect to your feelings for your father and your professional life, what I mean to say is you have some responsibility towards our relation also. You left me in so early days of our marriage and even after six months you were not ready to come back as you feel guilty to leave your paralyzed father alone.

But you are forgetting that your younger sister and your mother are also capable to take care of him. But they never took the responsibility as you were carrying their onus on your shoulder since years in every responsibility towards your father and even all family members.

We can even keep full time Nurse to take extra care of papa which will be supporting to him and to you also. We can give him proper medical care as well as enjoy at least some time together that's it."

With tears in her eyes Gauri asked Manish to forgive her for neglecting him and accepted to go with him same day. They made arrangements for her father immediately and Gauri moved with Manish to start her newly wedding life in a fresh way.

Many times we unknowingly keep ourselves over burdened by taking too many responsibilities which are no doubt important but can be taken care of by others for a while. When Understanding is strong between the partners Marriages can be saved at any point of time.

15

Tell me one more beautiful lie.

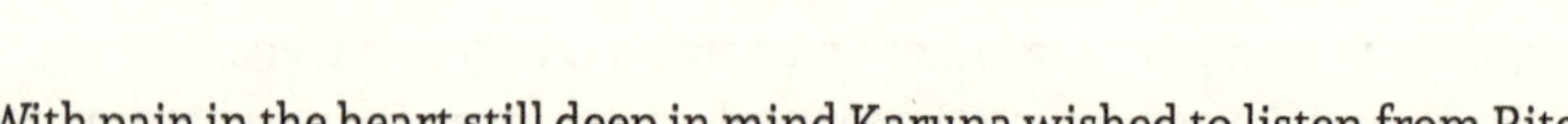

With pain in the heart still deep in mind Karuna wished to listen from Ritesh that he was telling one more beautiful lie, but in vain!

"Sorry Karuna, but this is the truth of our relation now. I can't stay with you anymore !"

Telling this to Karuna, Ritesh left for Bangalore as he had decided and planned for it. It was difficult for Karuna to understand and digest the situation so she called up her mother,

"Mumma, I need your presence here badly. I am all alone and don't know what to say, please come so that at least you will help me out to cope up with this mess."

Karuna's mother came to Mumbai to assist her in coming out from the shock Ritesh has given her. She could sense the coming miserable days for her daughter so she asked Karuna,

"This is not the time to repent on the decision taken in the past and not even waiting for the future to change on it's own. I will take care of my granddaughter and you should focus on starting your job again!"

Karuna was also knowing the need of the hour but she was not able to gather the confidence again. It was a long gap she was away from professional life. She was disturbed by the breakup Ritesh declared suddenly. Her mother briefed few things to me and fixed her appointment with me.

"Madam, I am totally blank now. Don't know how to tell you what reasons Ritesh has given me! He has an issue with my complexion and few patches on skin which were already present before our marriage. I agree that I have put on some weight after my delivery which can be reduced also. I just need some time for it. But how can I change my skin colour or remove patches from it?"

Karuna was asking me solution of many things at a time so I asked her to tell about them from the start.

" I was working as a CFO in a renowned firm in Bangalore. Ritesh was also woking in the same firm. We met each other after office many times. After knowing each other thoroughly we decided to get married and moved to Mumbai our dream city to live in. We spent good time with each other. We were earning well and had good amount of saving with us but now I am in financial crunch !" It was strange to hear from her so I asked Karuna,

" Your profile was good and as you told about initial days stability, I would like to know what went wrong that you have a financial crunch now?" With a helpless smile on her face she replied,

" I handed over all my savings to Ritesh for buying Luxury flat for us before thinking of baby planning. Those days were like we were one entity so never had separate bank accounts. As per need he used to take out money from it. The flat is registered on his name and now he wished to move in, in it so he asked me to vacate it. We have a baby girl who has a premature birth so doctors asked me to take special care. We both decided that I will focus on her and home for few years and Ritesh will take care of earnings."

Knowing the need of the hour our main purpose was to build up confidence in Karuna first so that she can survive better with her child. We took sessions to discuss how she can manage all again and what is her forte! To our pleasant surprise she regained it again and got her old job in the same firm. Her mother was there to take care of her kid. Later Karuna tried her best to discuss and convince Ritesh to patch up and come back again and finally she came to tell me,

" Madam, sorry to tell you that now I wish to move on in my life. I am ready to sign the divorce papers Ritesh has sent. We tried our best to bring him back but what I found is, he has lost that love, care, respect and even humanity for me. He is giving me false reasons till now but today he gave me the real reason that he has someone else in his life.

He told that I was focusing more on our daughter and not gave him attention so he lost interest in our relation which resulted in getting attracted towards his new life partner he has thought of. They are engaged with each other from last one year and I was foolishly trying to win his heart. He planned everything from leaving 6 months away to get divorced immediately and having the flat on his name. I will take legal help to take my finances back in my account. I can live happily with my daughter than begging a love which doesn't exist anymore."

The decision was tougher but Karuna was emotionally and mentally ready for that as she was not willing to listen lies from Ritesh anymore. Life doesn't stop for anyone so all were with Karuna to cheer her up in the decision she was forced to take.